SAYS WHO?

Sarah Elizabeth Randall

Tellwell Talent
www.tellwell.ca

ISBN
978-0-2288-6288-8 (Hardcover)
978-0-2288-4916-2 (Paperback)
978-0-2288-4917-9 (eBook)

Motivated by my amazing teacher
and friend Ann-Marie.

Inspired by the Jacaranda Class
at St Stephens Preschool.

Every Sunday morning
when Tom was free,
He would plan for an adventure
up his jacaranda tree.

He would ransack his sister's closet
and fancy dress chest;
He would make an almighty mess until
he liked how he was dressed.

Today was a hit with bumble-striped
tights and a polka dot skirt.
Tom wasn't a fan of football jerseys
and being covered in dirt.

His sister yelled out, "Tom, take them off and put them away; what on earth would the other boys say?

They are for girls, and not for you."
Tom replied, "Yeah? Says who?

I am who I am and I love what I see, I will wear these stripes and dots to climb my jacaranda tree!"

Tom scaled the jacaranda tree through
a tunnel of purple flowers.
Up in this tree, Tom imagined his mystical powers.

Anything he wanted to be,
his imagination would ignite:
a mermaid, a wizard, or a tall handsome knight.

He shimmied to the top, shouting,
"I am the queen of this castle. Be gone with
you, dragons; you are causing me hassle."

Tom heard the yells of his mother,

"Tom, it is time for your bath."

As he descended to the bottom, he heard a loud laugh.

At the foot of the jacaranda tree kids from

school were pointing and staring.

Karen shouted, "Tom, what on earth are you wearing?"

"You are dressed like a girl;
those things are not meant for you."
Tom replied, "Oh yeah? Says who!?
I am who I am, and I love what I see. I will wear my
stripes and dots to climb my jacaranda tree!"

The next day, Tom stood in his sister's
bumble-striped tights by the school gates.

He was waiting for Sam; they are the greatest of mates.

Sam is adopted; he has two dads.
He is handsome and witty, a real Jack of the lads.

Tom said, "Two dads. Leaping lizards; that is cool.
I see them most days dropping Sam off at school.
Reggie is always travelling; he is a famous soccer player.
Charlie stays at home, he is the laundry slayer."

Then piped up Karen, right on cue
"Two dads, that is weird!"
Sam said, "Oh yeah, says who?!

Oh, hush up, Karen, with your mindless chit chatter.
As long as they love me, what does it matter?"

That evening Sam was having a huge birthday bash.
Tom was so excited rummaging through
his sister's fancy dress stash.
To Tom's delight, he found Sam's birthday gift: a second
pair of bumble-striped tights still fresh in the packet.
Tom's mum screeched up the stairs:
"Tom, what is all that racket?"

"Mum, can I take these for Sam?
We can be twins! Peas in a pod."
Mum rasped "Tom they are for girls,
do you not think you will look rather odd?"

Tom gasped "Says who!?"

The party was a hit, Sam wore his matching
striped tights. What a trooper.
But then who showed up? A big party pooper!

Karen: a nightmare in a dress, the queen
of mean, the ultimate villainess.

"Oh, what a pair of sights. You look like girls prancing around in bumble-striped tights.

How strange, how odd, how utterly bizarre.
Boys should be covered in mud playing
with drums or a remote-control car."

Sam hissed "Says who?"

Karen's words hurt Tom; they made his tummy
fill with worry. He ripped off his stripes and
ran across the road, home in a hurry.

Sam raced to Tom's bedroom, up the jacaranda tree,
"ARRRGH, let's play pirates. I will be
Hook; you can be Tiger Lily"

Tom packed away his bumble-striped tights, under his bed.
"Why are you doing that?" said Sam, stroking Tom's head.
Tom's eyes filled up, and a tear rolled down his cheek, as
he whispered the words he had been too scared to speak.

"I don't like to get muddy and fight like other boys do.
Am I strange because I don't like the colour blue?"

"I dream of being a mermaid, brushing
my golden locks with a fork.
I imagine being a fashion designer for the London catwalk.

Imagine me in all those showbiz lights,
strutting my stuff in my bumble-striped tights."

Drawing his sword to stop Tom's tear,

Sam held out his hand and said, "Hey Tom, come here.

Look in the mirror and repeat after me:

I am who I am, and I love what I see.

I will wear my stripes and dots to climb my jacaranda tree!

Toms smile went from ear to ear and all the
worry in his tummy floated away.
Throwing on his stripes "play pirates did you say"?

Sam replied "you name it pirates, mermaids, wizards even giants! Let's go back to the party we are the bumble stripe alliance".

And off they shot out the window down the jacaranda
tree, from the bottom branch who should they see?
Karen's face full of shame holding up a pair of stripe
tights "can I please join in your game? I am sorry
that I hurt you both I only meant to tease, I think
you guys look kind of neat the real bees knees".

The boys slid to the bottom from a purple flower train. Tom helped Karen into her striped tights. He winked and said "now would you look at us we are all so different yet the same".

Lightning Source UK Ltd.
Milton Keynes UK
UKHW051137170921
390716UK00002B/33